Val,
Congratulations. :)
Katalin
& Val. G.

Love Song for a Baby

By **Marion Dane Bauer**
Illustrated by **Dan Andreasen**

SIMON & SCHUSTER BOOKS FOR YOUNG READERS
New York London Toronto Sydney Singapore

SIMON & SCHUSTER BOOKS FOR YOUNG READERS
An imprint of Simon & Schuster Children's Publishing Division
1230 Avenue of the Americas, New York, New York 10020

Book design by Paula Winicur
The text of this book is set in Kennerley.
The illustrations are rendered in oil on gessoed board.
Printed in Hong Kong

6 8 10 9 7

Library of Congress Cataloging-in-Publication Data

Bauer, Marion Dane.
Love song for a baby / by Marion Dane Bauer ; illustrated by Dan Andreasen.
p. cm.
ISBN 0-689-82268-5
1. Infants—Juvenile poetry. 2. Children's poetry, American.
[1. Babies—Poetry. 2. American poetry.] I. Andreasen, Dan ill. II. Title.
PS3552.A8363 L68 2002
811'.54—dc21   00-063535

For Bailey Dane Bataille, from Nonny —M. D. B.

To my children —D. A.

Come, my darling.
Come, my dear.
Come hear a song about a baby,
a very special baby.
Come hear a song about you.

Before the first stars blazed in your sky,
before the sun ever kissed you,
before you cried your first cry,
we loved you.

When you came into our arms,
slippery as salmon,
puckered as prunes,
loud as a lion,
already we knew,
we loved you.

You had tiny hands
with perfect nails
and fingers like the petals of a flower.
And yes,
we loved you.

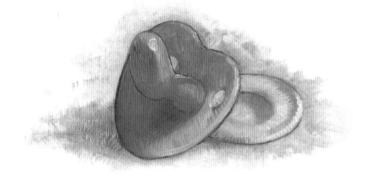

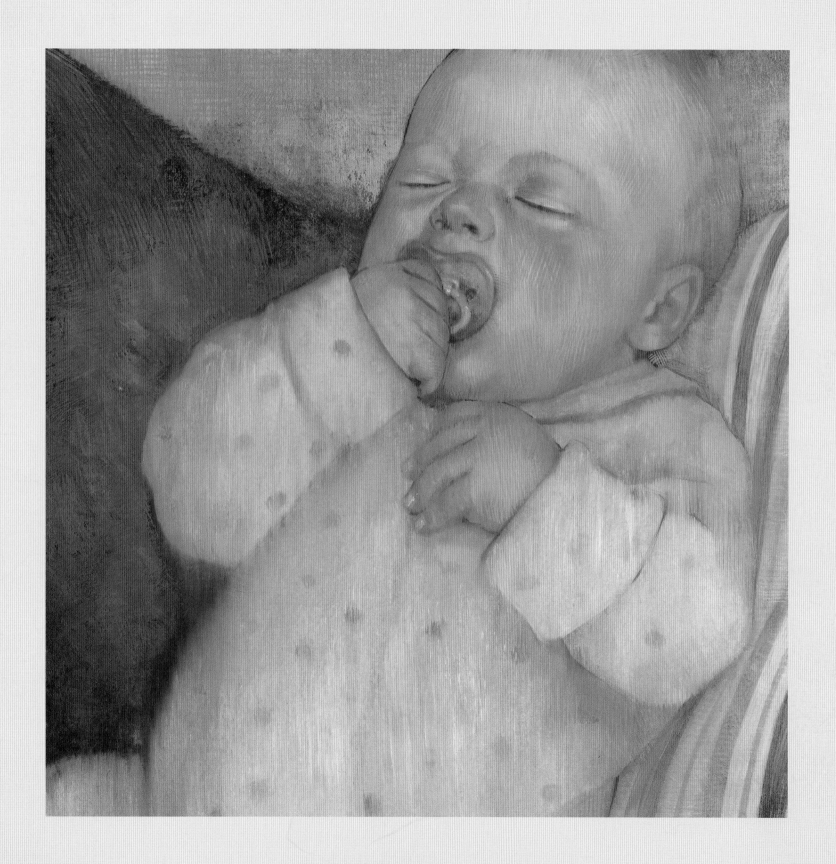

You came complete
with ten little toes
as sweet and pink as candies.
Certainly,
we loved you.

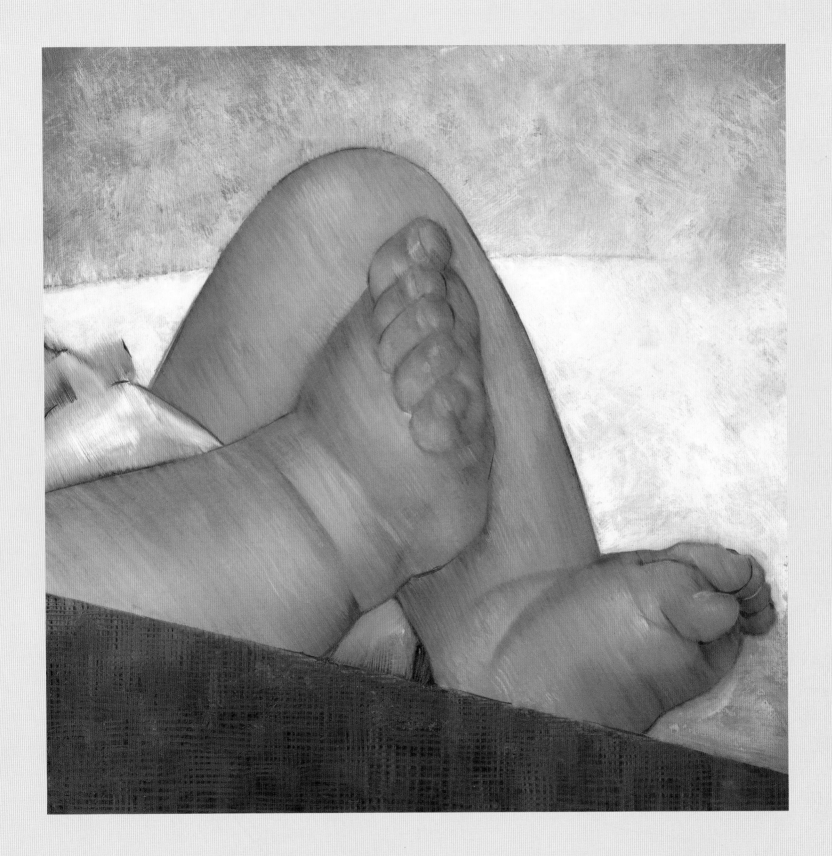

You had two eyes
and one very small nose,
not much hair,
and no teeth at all.
Still,
we loved you.

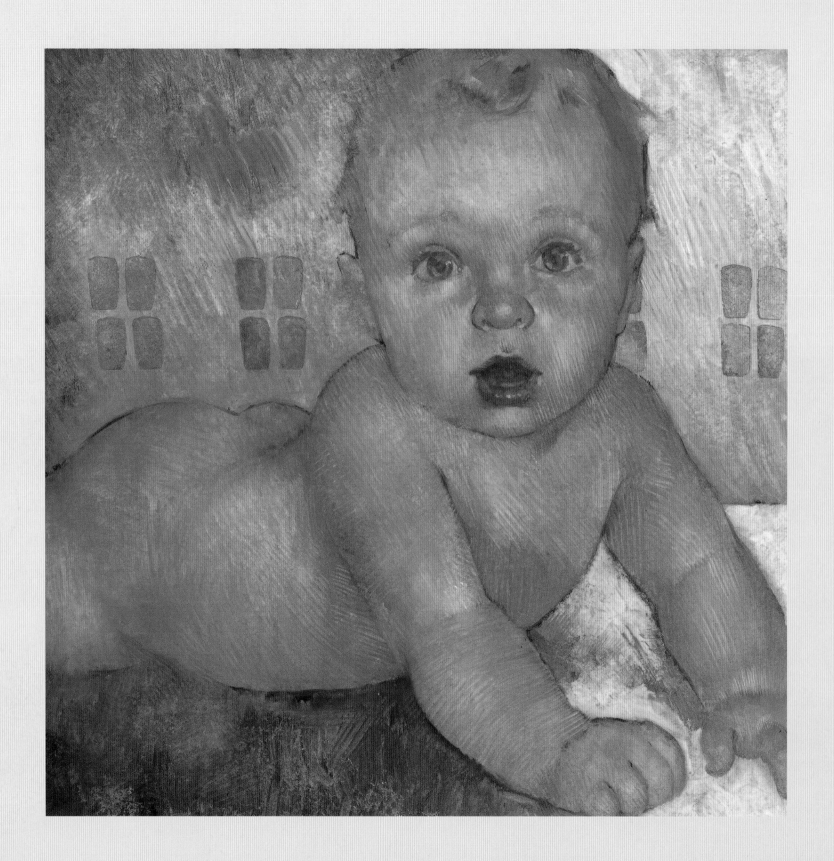

Round cheeks,
a round tummy,
a round little bottom,
all made us
love you.

Your laughter was the sun.
Your smile, the moon.
Even your burps were bells,
since
we loved you.

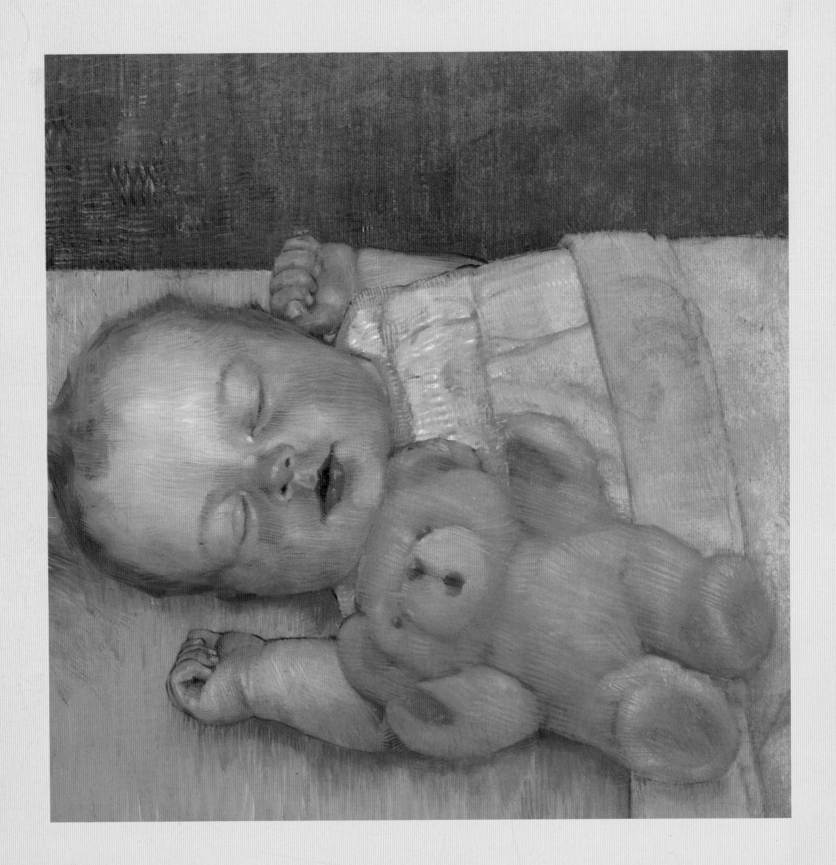

So we snuggled you,
we juggled you,
we watched you while you slept,
because it's true,
we loved you.

We clapped with you,
we danced with you,
we dried your tears
and soothed your fears.

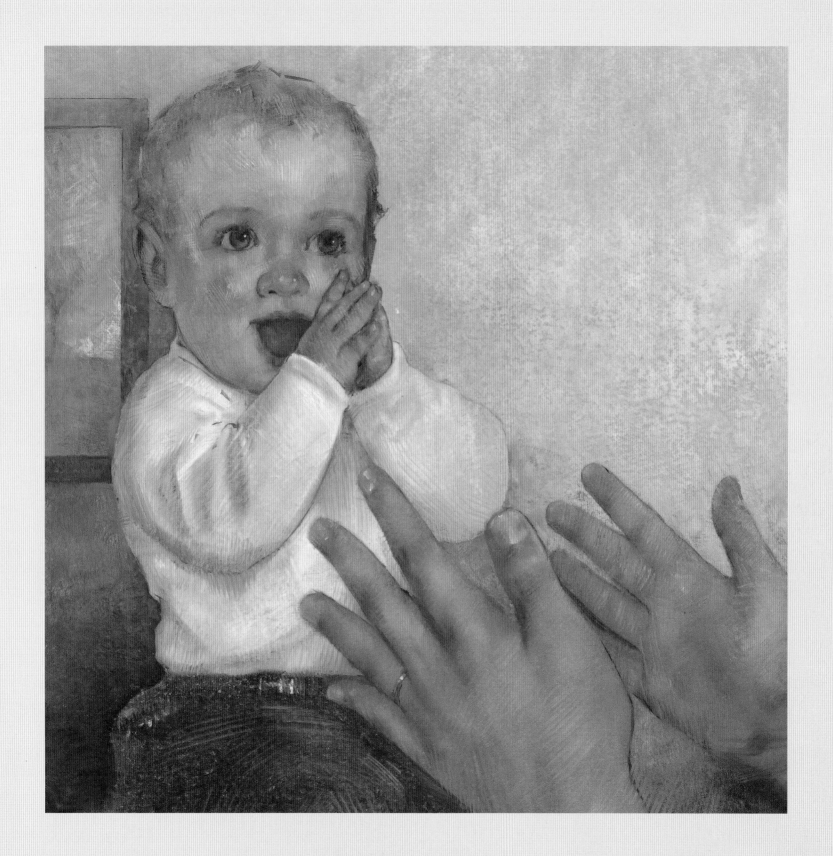

We tossed you high,
we kept you dry.
Can you guess why?
We loved you.

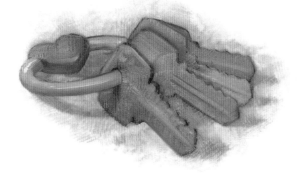

You burst upon our world like a comet,
like birdsong
in the silver silence of dawn,
and how could we help
but love you?

We'd dreamed a baby,
we'd wanted a baby,
we'd planned for a baby,
we'd waited and waited and waited
for a baby,
until finally,
there was you.

And oh,
how we love you!